W9-BVB-200

OTHER KIPPER BOOKS

Where, Oh Where, Is Kipper's Bear?

Kipper's Book of Numbers

Kipper's Book of Opposites

Kipper's Book of Colors

Kipper's Book of Weather

Kipper's Toybox

Kipper's Birthday

Copyright © Mick Inkpen 1996

All rights reserved. No part of this publication may be reproduced
or transmitted in any form or by any means, electronic or mechanical,
including photocopy, recording, or any information storage and retrieval
system, without permission in writing from the publisher.

Requests for permission to make copies of any part of the work should
be mailed to: Permissions Department, Harcourt Brace & Company,
6277 Sea Harbor Drive, Orlando, Florida 32887-6777.

First U.S. edition 1996
First published 1996 by Hodder Children's Books,
a division of Hodder Headline plc, 338 Euston Road, London NW1 3BH

Library of Congress Cataloging-in-Publication Data
Inkpen, Mick.
Kipper's Snowy Day/Mick Inkpen.—1st U.S. ed.
p. cm.
Summary: Kipper the dog spends the day enjoying
the snow with his best friend Tiger.
ISBN 0-15-201362-8
[1. Dogs—Fiction. 2. Snow—Fiction.] I. Title.
PZ7.I564jk 1996
[E]—dc20 95-47126

A C E F D B

Printed in Hong Kong

KIPPER'S SNOWY DAY

MICK INKPEN

E

Harcourt Brace & Company

San Diego   New York   London

DISCARDED

OIL CITY LIBRARY
2 CENTRAL AVENUE
OIL CITY, PA. 16301

It was a new morning
and it was snowing!
Huge cotton ball snowflakes were
tumbling past Kipper's window.

"Yes!" said Kipper, jumping out
of his basket. "Yes! Yes!"

He grabbed his scarf and wound
it three times around his neck.
"Yes! Yes! Yes!"

Kipper was very positive
about snow.

OIL CITY LIBRARY
2 CENTRAL AVENUE
OIL CITY, PA. 16301

Kipper rushed outside. The snow
lay deep and smooth and new, like an
empty page waiting to be scribbled on.
He made a paw print and then another.

And then with a whoop he went charging around and around, crisscrossing this way and that, until the garden was full of his tracks.

Kipper stopped to catch his breath, letting the swirling snowflakes melt on his tongue. Then he fell backward into the snow and lay there panting.

When he stood up, he found that he had made a perfect Kipper-shaped hole. He tried again. Then he tried a different shape. And another.

"I bet Tiger hasn't thought of this," he said, and ran off to find his best friend.

Kipper found Tiger at the top of Big Hill. He was wrapped up in a fat bundle of silly, woolly clothes. Kipper plopped a friendly snowball on top of his head.

"Hello," said Tiger.

Tiger pointed up at the sky. A watery sun was seeping through the gray clouds.

"It won't last," he said. "It'll all be gone by tomorrow. There's a warm wind coming." Tiger was like that. He knew about things.

Bout this was not at all what
Kipper wanted to hear, so he started
throwing snowballs at his friend.
     Tiger was very easy to hit
because the silly, woolly clothes were
wrapped so tightly around him that
he could hardly move.
And his own snowballs
stuck like little pom-poms
to the silly, woolly
gloves.

"Look at my new game," said Kipper, falling backward into the snow.

"You get up very carefully... and there you are!" And there he was, or at least the shape of him.

Tiger stretched out his arms, and fell backward with a soft, woolly *crump*. But when he tried to get up, he could not. He was too round. He just lay there waving his arms and legs like a beetle on its back.

Tiger heaved himself over onto his tummy, but rolled too far, and found himself on his back again. He tried again. The same thing happened. Snow began to stick in thick lumps to the silly, woolly clothes. Crossly, he heaved himself over once more.

This time he rolled over twice, three times, four times...

Slowly at first,
and then a little faster,
and then a lot faster,
and then very fast indeed,
Tiger rolled down the hill.

And as he went the silly, woolly
clothes picked up more and more
snow, so that by the time he
reached the bottom he had changed
from a small dog into a giant
snowball. The giant snowball
fell to pieces.

K ipper charged down the hill.
"Are you all right Tiger?" he panted.
Tiger pulled off his silly, woolly hat.
A big grin spread across his face.
"Again!" he said.

So that is what they did, all day long, taking turns to wear the silly, woolly clothes.

And by the time the sun began to dip toward the hill, making their shadows long and skinny, Kipper and Tiger had rolled enough snow to the bottom to build a giant snow dog.

They watched their shadows lengthen and fade.

"It'll all be gone by tomorrow," said Tiger. "There's a warm wind coming."

But for once
Tiger was wrong.
The warm wind stayed
away, and that night
another snowstorm smoothed out all
of Kipper's paw prints, making the
garden like a clean, white, empty
page once more.

And the snow dog stood at the
bottom of Big Hill wearing Tiger's
silly, woolly clothes...

for almost three...   whole...

weeks.